Joel Finds A Home

Other Books by Terry Parker

A Shepherd's Christmas Story
Sarah's Easter Miracle
The Camel Driver's Helper

Joel Finds A Home

by
Terry Parker
Illustrated by Sarah Grace Wright

F **W**
Fitting Words

Joel Finds a Home

Copyright © 2022 by Terry Parker

Isaiah 35:5–6 scripture is taken from The Holy Bible, English Standard Version® (ESV®)

Copyright © 2001 by Crossway, a publishing ministry of Good News Publishers. All rights reserved.

Publishing services provided by Fitting Words LLC—www.fittingwords.net

Illustrations by Sarah Grace Wright
Cover design provided by LAcreative - www.lacreative09.com

ISBN: 979-8-9871314-0-4

Library of Congress Control Number:

Printed in the United States of America

This story is dedicated to the many parents who have had the God-given privilege of raising a child like Joel. May this tale encourage you and your child.

Table of Contents

Chapter 1

Joel was a happy child. He liked sheep, goats, dogs, camels, and especially people. He loved to sing, laugh, run, and play, and he rarely looked sad. Except when he saw that someone else was sad or when he noticed someone being mean to another person. When he saw that happening, he would go up to the bully and tell that person to say sorry for being mean. He would then go over to the person who had been wronged, offer up a big hug, and say, "Don't worry—everything is going to be okay." That was just who Joel was.

Joel never knew his mother and father. For as long as he could remember, he had been passed from family to family, and he didn't stay long enough with any family to feel like where he lived was really his home. He knew that he would only be at each place for a short time before he would be picked up by another family.

Joel also didn't know what he looked like because he never saw himself in a mirror. No one except the Romans had mirrors. But he often heard what others had to say about him.

"Look how different Joel's eyes are. And his nose is different too," they would say. "And look at the funny way he moves his mouth from time to time."

He knew he looked different in some way from other children, but that didn't bother Joel at all. In God's eyes he was a perfect child, and that was the only thing that mattered to him.

Joel didn't know his exact age, but from what the families he stayed with said, and because of his size when he was around other children, he thought he must be twelve or thirteen years old. But he was always more comfortable playing with children who were a little younger, like the seven- or eight-year-olds.

Today was going to be a special day for Joel. He called it a "surprise day" because the family he had been living with for the last year was going to help him pack a small basket filled with all his clothes and other things, then leave him on the steps of the temple. It would be a big "surprise" for Joel to find out who his new family would be.

Joel loved being at the temple because he knew that God lived in the temple. And talking to God from the steps of the temple made Joel feel that God was especially close to him. Another reason Joel liked being on the steps of the temple was because one of his very favorite people was always there, sitting on the bottom step and begging for food or money. The man had told Joel that he was lame, which meant that he couldn't walk.

"Hi, Old Man," Joel said as he came to sit beside his friend. Joel called him Old Man because once when Joel asked for his name, the beggar had simply answered that everyone called him Old Man. That was just fine with Joel, and Old Man liked it, too, as he knew he was older than most everyone who passed by. He said he used to wonder why God allowed him to live so long, but now he was simply proud of his age and believed that God had a plan for him. He couldn't wait to find out what that plan was.

"Are you having a good day, Old Man?" Joel asked.

"No," Old Man said. "It is really cold today, and I don't have a coat to keep me warm."

"I'd give you my coat," Joel said, "but it would be much too small for you. So why don't you just ask God to give you one?"

"I don't think God has an extra coat lying around," Old Man said.

"That is silly," Joel said. "God owns everything because He made everything. So I'm sure He made a coat for everyone. And one of those coats was made especially for you. All we have to do is go find where God put your coat."

"Well, I think God forgot where He put my coat. And I sure don't know where it is," Old Man said.

"I'll tell you what, Old Man," Joel said. "You watch my things, and I'll go find where God put your coat." And with that, Joel stood up and skipped down the street in search of Old Man's coat.

The first place Joel came to was the bakery shop around the corner from the temple. There, down a narrow side street, a woman was selling date cakes.

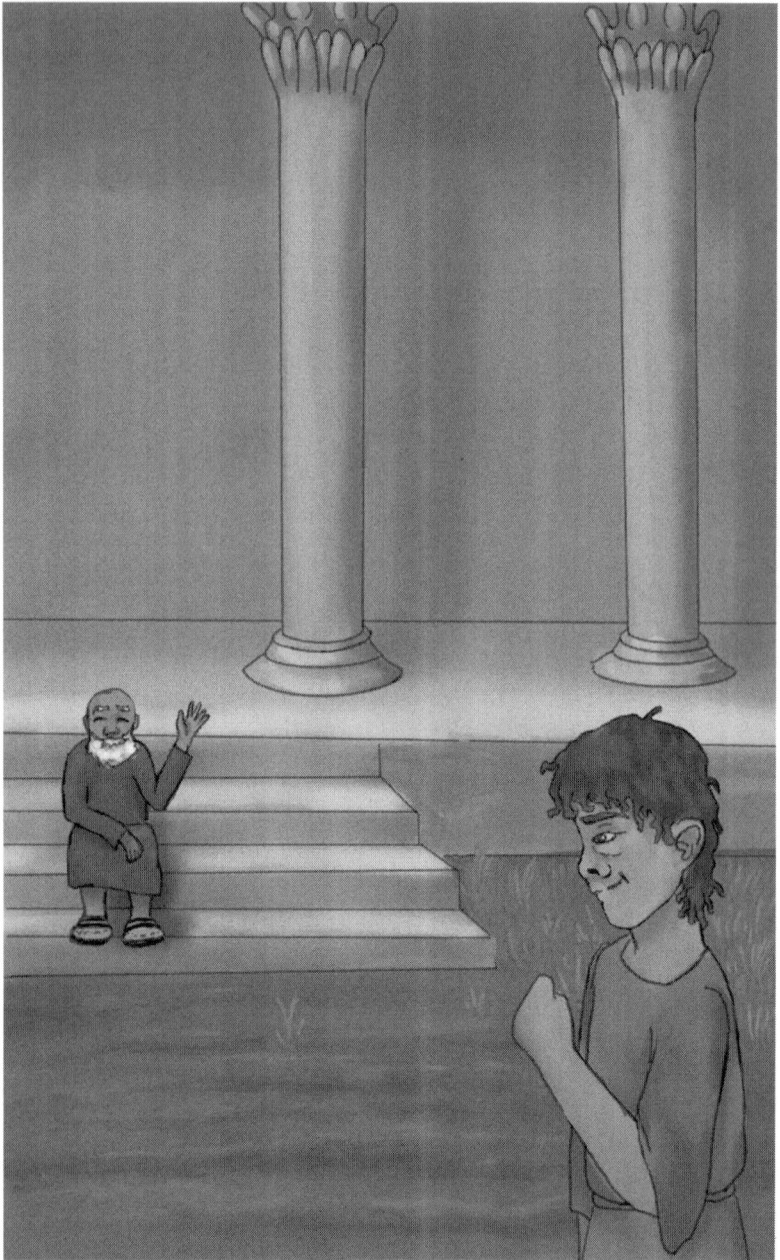

"Can you help me?" Joel asked the baker.

"I'm not sure if I can or not," the baker said. "What is it that you want?"

"I'm looking for Old Man's coat," Joel said. "He needs it badly because it is so cold today."

"Well, he didn't leave it here," the baker said, "as I don't see any coats lying around my shop." She looked Joel up and down and then asked, "Why did you think it would be here? Did Old Man say he left it here?"

"Oh no," Joel said, "you know he can't walk. He just sits at the bottom step of the temple all the time."

"I know," the baker said. "When I go to the temple, I often take him some of my leftover date cakes. But he's never been in my shop."

"Even though he doesn't come here," Joel said, "I thought God might have left Old Man a coat here for me to pick up."

"Well, God didn't leave any coats here," the baker said. "But I wouldn't mind if God would leave a bunch of dates here. I'm almost out of dates, and our date palm trees are all picked bare. If I don't get some more dates to sell, I will not be able to feed my family, and I'll have to close my shop."

"So you need a miracle," Joel said, "just like Old Man needs a miracle. If you will pray that I find Old Man's coat, I will pray that God will send you more dates."

And with that, Joel ran down the street, continuing his search for where God might have left Old Man's coat.

The next place he stopped was at the wine merchant's shop. When he went inside, the merchant looked up and said, "Aren't you in the wrong shop, little boy? Or did your parents send you to pick up some wine for dinner?"

"Oh no," Joel said, "I don't want any wine—and I don't have any parents. It was God who sent me here."

"Oh my goodness," the wine merchant said. "Why on earth would God send you to a poor wine merchant like me? I haven't talk to God in years."

"My, my," Joel said. "Why haven't you talked to God in years? I bet that makes Him very sad."

"Well, I guess I've just been too busy," the wine merchant said. "And besides, why would God want to talk to me, anyway?"

"That's an easy question to answer," Joel said. "God cares about everyone, including you. And God loves it when people talk to Him. And you could thank Him for giving you grapes to make wine. And you could ask Him for more grapes if you need them."

"I don't need any more grapes," the wine merchant said. "But I really need some new wineskins. The ones I have are old, and the new wine I put in them keeps busting out and leaking as the wine ages."

"Well, I'll ask God to send you some new wine skins if you will help me find where God left Old Man's coat," Joel said.

"Sorry," the wine merchant said. "I don't know this Old Man person, and I certainly don't have his coat."

"Okay, thanks," Joel said. And with that, he turned and ran farther down the street.

*   *   *

From the door of his shop, the wine merchant watched Joel go and said to himself, "Now that's about the strangest thing that has happened to me in quite a while." As he turned to go back inside, he added, "Maybe I really ought to ask God to send me some wineskins. And I guess I'll ask him to send Old Man a coat too. It certainly couldn't hurt."

*   *   *

Just then Joel approached the next shop on the street and stopped in his tracks. "Of course," he said to himself. "Why didn't I think of that before? This had to be where I'll find Old Man's coat." The shop had all kinds of clothes hanging outside on the hooks along the wall. It was a clothes shop, where people came for pants, shirts, and, of course, coats. Joel ran inside. As soon as he saw the tailor standing behind a table with a needle and thread in his hand and a bolt of cloth laid in front of him, Joel said in a loud voice, "Boy, am I glad to see you!"

"And why would that be?" the tailor asked as he looked at Joel with surprise.

"Because I came to get Old Man's coat," Joel said.

"Well, who is this Old Man?" the tailor asked. "And when did he order a coat?"

"He didn't order a coat," Joel said. "God ordered the coat for him."

"Oh, is that so?" the tailor said. "And why didn't God tell me about this coat?"

"Maybe you weren't listening," Joel said.

"Of course I listen to God," the tailor said. "I go to the temple every Sabbath, and I listen to the rabbi teach and read from the scriptures all the time. And everyone knows God speaks to us from the scriptures," he added.

"That's what I always tell my families," Joel said. "But they sometimes aren't as wise as you. They don't always understand that God is speaking to them through the scriptures."

"So, what does that have to do with an Old Man and a coat?" the tailor asked.

"Well," Joel said, "didn't the teacher John the Baptist say that we should give to the poor, and that if we have two coats and our brother has no coat, we should give him one of ours?"

"I suppose so," the tailor said, not sure where all of this was leading. "But I don't know any poor people. All of my friends are well-off."

"You say you go to the temple all the time," Joel said. "Don't you remember the lame man who sits on the bottom step?" Without waiting for the answer, he added, "Well, he is poor—so you know at least one of the poor that John the Baptist mentioned."

While the tailor was thinking about what Joel had said, Joel continued, saying, "Old Man doesn't have any coat at all, and you don't just have two coats—you have lots and lots of coats that are hanging up outside and inside your shop."

With that, Joel stopped and waited for the tailor to say something. Finally, he did.

"Well, I guess I have an older coat in the back that I can give you for Old Man."

"But, Mr. Tailor, that wouldn't be too smart," Joel said.

"Why not?" the tailor said.

"It says in Proverbs that he who gives to the poor lends to the Lord, and the Lord will repay. So it seems to me that if you give Old Man an old coat, then the Lord will repay you with an old blessing. But just think, if you give Old Man a brand-new coat, then the Lord will repay you with a brand-new blessing," Joel said.

"You know, you are exactly right, little boy," the tailor said. "It would be really nice to receive a brand-new blessing from the Lord."

So the tailor took a brand-new coat off the wall and handed it to Joel to give to Old Man. Then the tailor said to tell Old Man that the tailor had been holding this coat just for him, and that he was glad Old Man had finally sent someone to pick it up.

Before he left the shop, Joel asked, "What new blessing can God send you?"

"Well," the tailor said, "business has been kind of slow, except for a request I've received from the wine merchant. Unfortunately, I don't have the material I need for his order. So I guess

I need more business or the material to make things for the wine merchant."

"What does the wine merchant want?" Joel asked, even though he thought he knew the answer.

"He wants me to sell him some new wineskins, but I don't have any goatskins available that I can use to make the wineskins," the tailor said. "And," he added, "I can't find any from my normal sources."

"Well, I will pray that God will send you some new goatskins," Joel said.

Then, with the coat in his arms, Joel ran back to the temple as fast as he could to give the new coat to Old Man. He told Old Man what the tailor had said, and the two of them sent a prayer up to God right then and there, asking God to bless the tailor with a brand-new blessing of lots of goatskins. Joel also prayed for God to send the baker more dates, and Old Man prayed that God would send a special blessing to Joel as well.

And before the day was out, God sent Joel a very special blessing indeed.

Chapter 2

J oel stayed with Old Man for the rest of the morning, but no family came to get him. He wasn't worried, though, as this had happened before. He didn't really know how many families he had lived with over the years; he only knew that God always sent him to just the right ones. Some were better than others, but from what he had learned listening to the scriptures, he was sure that when the families weren't all that kind or loving, God was teaching Joel patience.

Toward the middle of the afternoon, as Joel was watching people come and go in front of the temple, he saw an interesting thing. Two boys were carrying a large wooden box down the middle of the street. Joel just had to find out where they were going and what in the world the box was for. So he jumped up from his seat on the steps and ran off in pursuit of the two boys. Old Man didn't pay him much attention; he had seen Joel do this many times before.

Joel followed the boys for what seemed like forever. Finally, they came to a campground just outside the city gates where there seemed to be fifty camels and just as many tents. He knew that people called this a "caravan of merchants." What a joy that was for Joel! Caravans go all over everywhere—to places Joel had dreamed about but never expected to visit. He couldn't wait to see what the two boys were going to do here.

*   *   *

"Come on, Daniel, keep holding up your end of the rack. I feel like I'm carrying the whole load," Amos said to his little brother. They had been on their way through the streets of Jerusalem to deliver a camel rack to one of the camel drivers who was camped out with the caravan. Their father, James, was a carpenter who made the wooden camel racks that were put on the backs of camels to help tie down goods.

"I think we are there now, Daniel," Amos said. "I see the flag that father said we should look for. The one with the dragon's head on it. It is high up on that pole straight ahead of us."

The two boys struggled hard not to drop the precious rack as they came up next to the camel that was standing by the flag.

"Well it's about time you got here," a rather rough-looking boy said. He was holding the bridle of one of the camels. "I've got more important things to do than wait on the likes of you. Now put that thing up on the camel, and let's see how it fits."

Amos was only fourteen years old, and the rough-looking boy appeared to be four or five years older. But Amos was strong for his size, and Daniel knew that Amos was not frightened by bullies.

"Daniel is too small to help lift the rack all the way up to the camel's back," Amos said to the bully, "so you will have to help me."

"Sorry, kid," the bully said, "I don't lift things with the hired help. If Shorty here can't help you, then you'll just have to do it yourself."

"Okay," Amos said. "If you're not going to help me put the rack up on the camel, then Daniel and I will just take the rack back to the shop. There are lots of other camel drivers who will buy this rack." Daniel and Amos picked up the rack and started back the way they had come.

"That's fine with me," the bully said.

Just then Joel saw a large man, with a long, scraggly beard, come running up to the boys. He was dressed in leather pants and holding a long whip.

"Here, here," he yelled. "What's going on?"

"We are taking our rack back to our father's shop because this bully won't help us put the rack on the camel's back, and I can't do it by myself," Amos said.

Upon hearing that, the large man went into a rage, and he turned his anger on the bully.

"You lazy servant!" he shouted. "I should give you a dozen lashes with this whip. I have paid a lot of money for this rack, and I don't want to lose it because you are too lazy to do your job."

He turned back to Amos and Daniel and said, "Boys, bring the rack back. Your father is the best carpenter in all of Judea, as was his father, Joseph, before him. No one makes a camel

14

rack as fine as he does. Why, all the other racks fall apart half-way across the desert. But your father's rack will stay sound for dozens and dozens of trips and outlast three camels. In fact, I need three more racks just like this one, and I want you to take this bag of shekels to your father and tell him if he can deliver them in two weeks, I'll pay him a shekel more for each one."

Then he turned to the bully and said, "Hold the camel steady." And all by himself, he picked up the rack like it weighed next to nothing and easily threw it up on the camel's back. "Now tie it down you lazy servant, while I go tend to some important business," he said. "And you boys give your father my thanks and my greeting, will you?"

Before Daniel and Amos could even answer, the man had gone.

The boys walked off a little way but turned back to watch the bully tie the straps under the camel. They wanted to be sure that the rack fit the camel well and was tied down correctly.

And Joel, from his hiding place behind a nearby tree, watched all of this take place. He wondered whether the camel would be okay with the rack on its back. He had never seen a camel carrying a big load, so he was not sure exactly what to expect.

* * *

As the bully tried to pull the straps under the camel to fasten them tightly, the camel kicked up his back leg, almost hitting the bully. He jumped away just in time, and, with a stick from the ground, he struck the camel hard on top of its head. The camel groaned in pain, and, at the same time, Joel sprang from his hiding place and ran over to the bully.

Loudly, Joel told the bully, "Say you are sorry."

"What did you say?" the bully asked.

"I said to tell the camel you're sorry," Joel said. And then he stepped over and hugged the camel's leg real tight.

"Are you crazy?" the bully shouted. "I don't say I'm sorry to camels when I hit them, and you'd better let go of that animal or he'll kick you so hard you will think a tree fell on you."

"He won't kick me," Joel said. "He likes me."

"Let him go!" the bully yelled. "Now!" he added as he raised his stick as if to strike Joel. But just then, since he wasn't paying attention to the camel, it struck out with its back leg and hit the bully on his arm, causing him to drop the stick, lose his balance, and fall to the ground. He then jumped up and started to move toward Joel.

*   *   *

On seeing all of this take place, Amos ran forward and stood between Joel and the bully.

"Don't you dare hit this boy," he said. "And don't hit the camel again either. If you do, I'll tell my father not to make any more racks for your master, and I know he won't like that."

The bully looked very worried. He clearly did not want to be whipped by his master. "Look," the bully said. "If I promise not to hit the camel again, will you take this crazy kid away and leave me alone?"

"It's a deal," Amos said. Then Amos and Daniel each took one of Joel's hands, and the three of them walked away.

As they reached the city gate, Joel turned to Amos and said, "Are you my new family?"

"What do you mean?" Amos asked.

"Well, I know God is sending me a new family today, so you must be it," Joel said.

"God didn't send us," Amos said.

"How do you know that?" Joel asked.

Not knowing exactly what to say in response, Amos decided to ask a couple more questions. "What about your mother and father?" he said. "And why do you need a new family?"

"I don't know who my mother and father are," Joel said, "so God just sends me families to take care of me for a while until He decides I have done enough for that family. Then He sends me a new family."

"So you don't have a family right now?" Daniel asked.

"No," Joel said. "The family I have had for the past year left me on the steps of the temple this morning and told me that God was sending me a new family."

"Oh, how exciting," said Daniel. "Do you think we can keep him?" Daniel asked Amos.

"I don't know," Amos said. "This is too big a question for us to answer by ourselves. And I don't want to just take him home to Father. So let's go ask Grandmother what we should do. She always knows what's right."

"Who is your grandmother?" Joel asked.

"Her name is Mary. And she is the mother of Jesus our Lord," Daniel said.

"And is she the mother of your father too?" Joel asked in amazement.

"That's right," Amos said.

"Then your father is the brother of Jesus," Joel said. "Wow," he added. "And Old Man says that Jesus is the Messiah."

This was too much for Joel to take in, so he kept thinking about what they had said as he went along with them.

In a short time, they came to a small house on a slight hill surrounded by a beautiful garden of fruits and flowers. As they entered the house, Amos and Daniel left him at the door and went across the front room to talk with a woman who was sitting in a rocking chair and sewing on a beautiful piece of cloth. After Amos talked with the lady, the two boys came back to Joel and told him that their grandmother wanted to talk to him.

So Joel went over and put his head in her lap. He said very softly, "I love you."

"I love you, too, Joel," she answered.

"How do you know my name?" Joel asked. "I never told those boys my name."

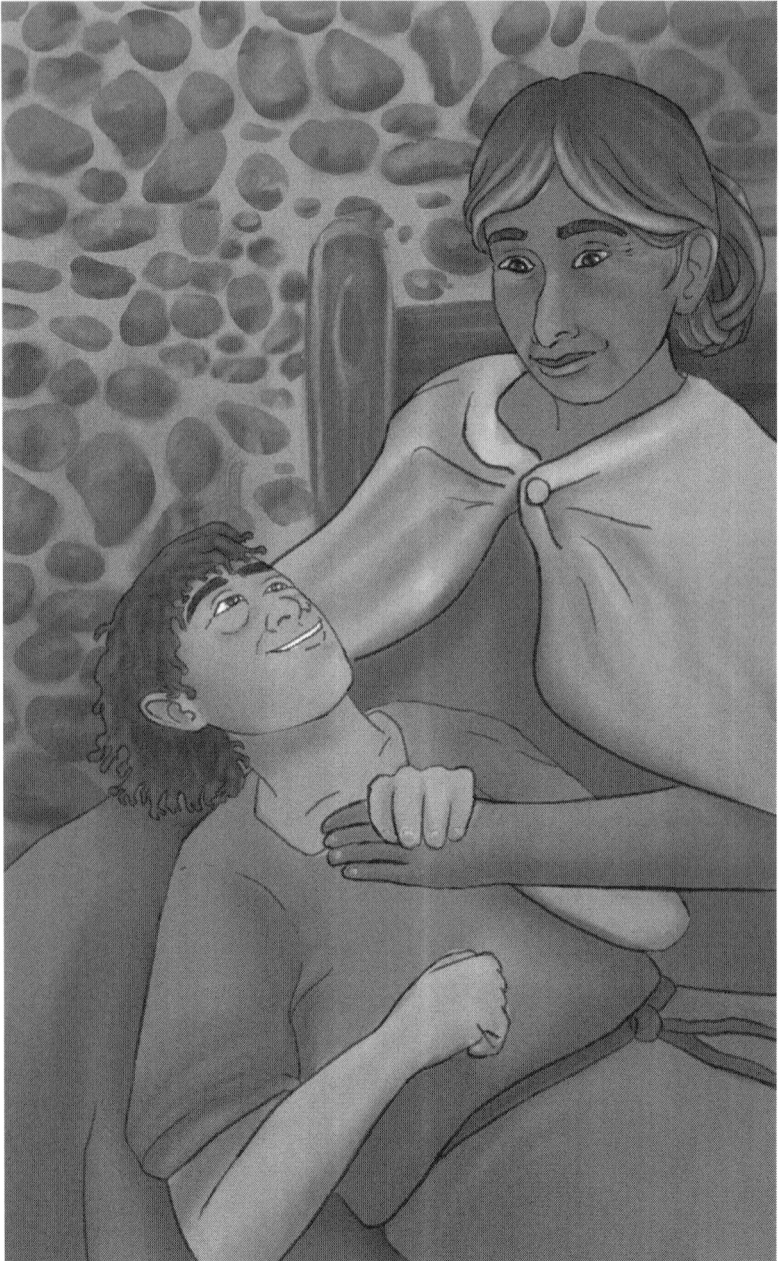

"God told me your name, Joel, and He told me I was going to get to meet you today."

"Are you really the mother of Jesus?" Joel asked.

"Yes," she said.

"So Jesus is their uncle?" Joel said, nodding his head toward Amos and Daniel.

"That is correct," Mary said.

"If I join their family, will Jesus be my uncle too?" Joel asked.

Mary answered, "Joel, Jesus will be, and is, much more to you than your uncle."

"I don't understand," Joel said.

"You will," Mary said. "You will. Now go home with Amos and Daniel. I've told them what they need to tell their father."

So off the boys went to the home of James the Carpenter.

Chapter 3

When Amos and Daniel got home, they went straight to the yard where their mother, Sarah, was working in the garden.

"And who do we have here?" Sarah asked when she saw Joel.

"He followed us home," Daniel said. "Can we keep him?"

"Well, that's not exactly right," Amos said. "We met him when we delivered the camel rack." Amos proceeded to tell their mother all that had happened and all that Joel had told them. The boys also told Sarah what their grandmother, Mary, had said.

Sarah said to the boys, "Okay, let me think about all of this. In the meantime, why don't you boys go and help your father clean up the shop? He has been hard at work all day, and the sawdust is everywhere from the work he has done on the furniture for the centurion."

As they went toward the building that was near the back of the house, Joel asked Amos, "What is a centurion?"

"He is a very important Roman soldier," Amos said. "He commands hundreds of other soldiers and is a very powerful person. He can arrest you and throw you in prison; or he can take all of your property for no reason at all."

"And he can even make you carry his packages for a whole mile if he wants to," Daniel added.

"Is he nice?" Joel asked.

"I don't know," Daniel said. "I've never had the nerve to talk to him."

"Well, you might get your chance today," a man who was standing in the door said. "The centurion is coming to pick up the piece of furniture that I made for him."

Upon seeing the man in the door, Amos said, "Oh, Father! I want you to meet Joel. We met him when we delivered the camel rack today."

Amos told their father everything that had happened to them and Joel at the camel driver's camp. But they didn't tell him what Joel had said to them about being Joel's new family. They also didn't tell their father what their grandmother, Mary, had said. They were going to let their mother do all that.

"Okay," James said. "You boys start cleaning the shop so it won't be such a mess when the centurion gets here. I'm going to go to the well and wash up."

*   *   *

JOEL FINDS A HOME

When James got to the well, Sarah was already there drawing water for her garden.

"Did you meet Joel?" Sarah asked.

"Yes," James said.

"Well, he tells me that we are supposed to be his new family," Sarah said.

"What is that supposed to mean?" James asked.

"It seems that because of the way he is, he has been passed from family to family his whole life. He doesn't even know who his real father and mother are," she said.

"Well, that can't be our problem," James said. "We will just have to take him back to whoever his last family was."

"We can't quite do that," Sarah said. "We don't know who they were, and he doesn't know either."

"That's ridiculous! He must have come from somewhere," James said.

"He came from the steps of the temple where his last family left him," Sarah said.

"Well, we can just take him right back and leave him on the steps of the temple," James said.

"Before you do that, I need to tell you a couple of things," Sarah said. "First, Joel says that God told him we are to be his next family and that God sent him to help you in particular."

"That is silly," James said. "How in the world can he help me?"

"I don't know," Sarah said, "but I also need to tell you what your mother, Mary, said about Joel."

"What! You mean my mother is in all of this and has already talked to Joel?"

"That's right," Sarah said. "And listen to what she said."

James sat down on the wall of the well. He knew that what he was about to hear was going to be very important since his mother said very few things. When Mary did speak, everyone listened because they all knew that she heard directly from God. Therefore, nothing Mary said could be taken lightly.

"Okay," James said. "What did my mother say?"

"She said that Joel is here to teach you some things God wants you to learn," Sarah said.

"Wow, that's a lot to think about," James said. "What in the world can a twelve-year-old boy, who acts like he is many years younger, teach me that I don't already know? And why a boy and not an adult—like a rabbi or a scribe or a teacher of the law? And how can he really know anything that I don't know? I surely don't want any of my friends to think that I don't know as much as a child."

"Maybe the first lesson is that God doesn't want us to be full of pride. Or to think we are smarter than we really are," Sarah said.

"That sort of stings," James said.

"And remember that Jesus said a young one shall teach them and God will use the meek and the lowly to teach the wise," Sarah said. "He also said that many who think they are wise are really foolish," she added.

"Well, if my mother said God sent him to teach me, I guess I'll have to go along with it for now, but I have my doubts," James said.

Just then James saw the centurion and a half-dozen guards come through the front gate. Normally, that many Roman soldiers coming through the gate would cause a lot of worry because the Romans controlled the country where James and his family lived. And sometimes soldiers came to arrest people that they thought were saying bad things about the Romans.

But James wasn't worried because the soldiers were there only to pick up the furniture he had made. They were not there to arrest anybody—at least that's what James hoped.

But he had never talked to the centurion personally. The furniture was ordered by one of the centurion's lieutenants. So James was ready to be on his best behavior—just in case.

However, as he walked forward to greet the centurion, he saw the new boy, Joel, come running out of the shop directly at the centurion. Before James could grab him and hold him back, Joel threw himself at the centurion, landing right on his breast plate, and into the centurion's outstretched arms.

James was horrified. He ran forward and, with his head bowed, said to the centurion, "I am so sorry. I hardly know this boy, and had I known he was going to do this, I would have kept him inside or held him back myself."

Even Sarah was standing there holding her hands to her mouth, frightened for what the centurion might do.

"It's okay," the centurion said to James. "Don't worry, you may not know Joel, but I am very well acquainted with him."

This surprised James so much that he was without words.

"Wow, you must really be important," Joel said. "James tells me that you can arrest people and throw them in prison."

Listening to Joel say that to the centurion made James even more uncomfortable, and again he had nothing to say.

"I am not any more important in God's eyes than you are, my little friend. And you know that as well as I do," the centurion said to Joel.

"That is because God loves us both just the same, doesn't He?" Joel said. It was more of a statement than a question.

"Yes, Joel, that's right," the centurion said.

With that, the centurion looked at James and said, "I guess a little explanation is in order." He set Joel down but continued to hold Joel's hand as he told James an amazing story.

"A little over a year ago, I was in the city with my ten-year-old son, Gaius. We got separated, and when I found him, he and Joel were deep in conversation. Gaius was explaining how our Master, Jesus, had healed him of a dreaded disease by simply telling me

that Gaius was made better because of my faith. Joel told Gaius and me that he loved Jesus too, and since then we all have been fast friends. Every time he can, Gaius plays with Joel in the city."

The centurion added, "Joel has taught me a thing or two over this past year. I bet he will teach you a thing or two as well. But I've talked enough about that—please show me the furniture that you have made for me."

James took the centurion into the shop and showed him the furniture. The centurion assured him that it would be the finest furniture in his house and thanked James for all the fine work. Then he and his soldiers loaded the furniture into their wagon.

Before they left, Joel gave the centurion one last hug. He waved to his friend as the centurion and his soldiers all left with the treasure.

James then turned to Joel and said, "Joel, why don't you eat dinner with us tonight? Then we will make you a bed with Amos and Daniel."

He didn't go so far as to say that they would be Joel's new family, but to the boys and Sarah, it certainly seemed that this was the case.

For the rest of the day, James couldn't stop thinking that maybe God had sent the centurion to him just to confirm what Mary had said. And maybe Joel was a special little boy who had something to teach James.

Over the next few weeks, he was going to find that out in a couple of amazing ways.

Chapter 4

Joel was very happy that God had sent him to this family. He could tell that they were going to need him to teach them some new things about the God they worshiped. Joel was ready to be God's instrument to do just that.

In fact, his work began the very next day.

The neighborhood they lived in was busy, and there were lots of children in the families surrounding their home and shop. Since James was the best carpenter in all of Judea, his work was in demand. So Amos and Daniel had to do lots of work around their father's shop, and they were constantly delivering things that their father had made.

They also gave Joel jobs to do—and Joel loved all of the jobs. Sweeping the sawdust on the floor was one of his favorite tasks. While he swept, he would sing songs.

"Why are you always singing?" Daniel asked one day.

"Because it is my way of thanking God for all He has given me," Joel responded.

"But God hasn't given you much of anything," Daniel said. "So what do you thank Him for?"

"Oh, you are wrong, Daniel," Joel said. "God has given me food to eat, clothes to wear, and families to live with. And He has given me the sun during the day and the moon and stars at night. And besides," Joel added, "even when I am cold or hungry or lonely, I thank God for all my troubles."

"Why in the world would you do that?" Daniel asked.

"Because God is teaching me to wait on Him. He shows me that I can't do any of these things without Him so that when He decides to go ahead and provide, I can give Him all the praise and thanks. And then when my next need comes, I will not have to worry because I know He will never let me want for anything."

"Wow, I don't know if I can do that," Daniel said. "But I do know I can count on my father and my mother to provide if God doesn't get around to it," he added.

"Daniel," his father said from his place at the workbench where he had been listening to the boys talk, "Joel is right. It is God that provides. As your father, I am merely God's instrument."

"What does that mean?" Daniel asked.

"It means that for each gift we receive, there is a person God uses to bring the gift to us. In our family, it is God who gives me the ability to make things I can sell for money. And if there is a shortage and we don't know where we will get the wood to make any more products, we always get on our knees and ask

God to provide. And because we know we can do that, and that He is the Creator of everything, we can have confidence that He will give us what we need."

"I like to think that God is never late in giving us what we need, and He's hardly ever early," Joel added.

"Well said, Joel," James said. "Now you boys get to work."

And off they went, with Daniel singing psalms right along with Joel.

*   *   *

After the boys had left, James sat down by the olive tree in the yard and thought about what Joel had said about thanking God for troubles. He understood that troubles often provided a chance to trust God for the outcome, but was that the only reason to thank God for troubles?

To come up with an answer, James thought back on as many times of troubles he could remember, and he came up with several things that now became clear to him.

First was the fact that God was in control of everything, so God was never surprised that James had troubles. God was aware of James's troubles even before James was.

Second, troubles always taught James patience—to wait on God for answers.

And third, he realized that the way he handled troubles was a good lesson to others about the nature of God.

So, just as Mary had said, Joel was teaching James things.

*   *   *

When they finished sweeping the sawdust from the workshop, Joel and Daniel went out into the garden to rest under the shade of a broom tree. Then Sarah came up with some fig cakes, fresh fruit, and a jug of water.

"Mother," Daniel said, "Joel wants to know if he can call you Mother. He says some of the other families he has lived with allowed him to do that, but sometimes they didn't. So he always asks first."

"Absolutely, Joel," Sarah said. "I would be glad for you to call me Mother."

Joel went over and gave Sarah a big hug. Then he looked up into her eyes and said "I love you, Mother."

"I love you, too, Joel," she answered. "Now hurry up and eat so you can get back to work."

When they got back to the shop, Joel went up to James and asked if he could call James Father. James looked down at him and said, "Joel, I don't think that is a good idea. Let's just see how things go for a while first."

"Okay," Joel said. "None of the other men in the families I've lived with ever allowed me to call them Father. Maybe God is not ready to let you do that, so I'll just pray that God will let you know if you will be the first one that lets me call you my father."

James just stood there with his mouth open, not knowing exactly what to say, while Joel ran off to help Daniel bring in some new wood for James to use in his furniture.

*   *   *

The next day James woke up all three boys early.

"Get up, you lazyheads. I need you to carry some ladders to the date farmers. I've loaded them in the wagon and hitched up Jeremiah, so the load is ready to go." Jeremiah was their faithful donkey who had been with the family for as long as the boys could remember.

"Jeremiah is amazing," Daniel told Joel. "He can pull the cart with all those ladders *and* with a water bag on the side of the cart, even if one of us happens to get in because we are too tired to walk. He is the strongest donkey I've ever seen."

So off they went with Amos leading Jeremiah, Daniel running behind the cart to be sure nothing fell off, and Joel riding on top of the load of ladders.

Before long, Joel saw up ahead rows and rows of date palm trees on both sides of the road. They went on as far as he could see.

"Praise God! Praise God! Thank You, Jesus! Thank You, Jesus!" Joel shouted.

"What are you yelling about?" Amos asked. "And don't be so loud. There are Roman soldiers up here, and we don't want to make them mad."

But Joel kept on shouting and praising the Lord. Hearing him, some of the Roman soldiers stopped what they were doing and came over to the cart.

"Well, I see you have brought us the ladders from James the Carpenter. Now pull over here so we can unload them," they said. "And tell that little boy to stop yelling."

As Amos led Jeremiah over to the date palm trees, Daniel leaned over to the cart and said in a low voice, "Joel, stop yelling. You are going to get us all in a lot of trouble."

"Oh Daniel, when I see God work His miracles, I can't help but shout about it," Joel said. And with that, he let out the loudest shout of all his praises, causing everyone to stop what they were doing and stare at him.

Just then a soldier who seemed to be in charge came riding over on a big stallion. Amos and Daniel immediately hid behind the cart, not knowing exactly what to do. But to their amazement, the soldier stopped by the cart, leaned over, and took Joel's hand. "Joel, my young friend," he said. "Can you please tell us all why you are praising God?" It was the centurion again.

"Oh Mr. Centurion, I'm so glad it's you," Joel said. "None of these others will understand, but you saw God's miracle when your son was healed by Jesus. Now I'm going to see my prayer answered just like you did."

Amos and Daniel couldn't believe their eyes and ears. They listened in amazement as Joel continued.

"Mr. Centurion, there is a baker in the city who sometimes gives Old Man, who is lame, some leftover date cakes to eat. I saw her a few days ago, and she said she has used up all of the dates on her trees. I told her I would pray that God would send her more dates. And now today I see tree after tree after tree full of dates. I know you have extra dates—more than enough to feed your men—so you are the answer to my prayer. Now you can tell everyone God not only answered your prayer, but also used you to answer somebody else's prayer."

"Well, Joel, when you put it that way, I guess I have no choice but to give you our extra dates," the centurion said. And with that, he ordered his men to load the cart with dates after they unloaded the ladders.

Once that was all done, and the children had started back, Amos looked at Joel and asked, "Okay, Joel, do you know what we are supposed to do with all these dates? I don't think Father will be too pleased if we bring them home."

"Don't worry," Joel said. "I know exactly where we are supposed to take them." Then he told Amos and Daniel where they could find the baker in town who had run out of dates.

When they arrived at the baker's shop, she was sitting in a chair outside. She saw Joel and the cart completely full of dates. And when she found out that the dates were all for her, she grabbed Joel's hands, and the two of them danced and danced around in circles, praising God. Daniel and Amos joined them, too, and they all danced until none of them could even stand up.

JOEL FINDS A HOME

When they were leaving the baker, Joel hugged her and said, "I love you." She told him she loved him too—and she promised Joel that the first thing she was going to do was bake a dozen date cakes for Old Man. This pleased Joel greatly.

When the boys got home, they couldn't stop talking about all that had happened to them that day.

*   *   *

After listening to their story that night, James went out into the moonlight and talked to his brother Jesus in prayer. He asking Jesus to show him how he could have the same faith that Joel had.

Chapter 5

F or the next several weeks, there was a lot of work to do
around the shop. A new caravan was camped outside the
gates of Jerusalem, and the head camel driver of over one
hundred camels was having a hard time with his wooden racks.
Many of the racks had broken so badly along the trip that the
only thing they were good for was firewood. When the camel
driver had learned of a skilled carpenter in Jerusalem who
made racks that would not break apart, he sent a messenger to
ask James to make twenty-five new racks.

James and Amos, with the help of Daniel and even Joel, who
had learned how to sand the wood until it became smooth,
completed thirty racks. They were in the last stages of putting
on the straps when the caravan arrived.

A lot of work went into making all these camel racks. Here's
what the process involved:

First, Daniel, Amos, and Joel had to go all over the countryside
around Jerusalem to gather wood—mostly olive wood—from
old trees that had been cut down or had died. Most of the time
the landowners let them have the wood for free just to get rid

of it. Sometimes James would trade a chair or a table for the wood.

When they got the wood into the shop, James and the boys—and other workers James hired from time to time—would cut the wood into strips that were just the right length and width. For a camel rack, James had to build a frame the exact shape of a camel's back so that it could fit on top of a blanket thrown over the camel and would stay in place no matter which way the camel moved. This frame was held together by straps made from animal skins. Goatskins were the strongest. James was especially skilled at using the straps to hold the frame together so it wouldn't break down, even after many trips.

Then James would build four sides onto the frame. These sides could hold whatever load the camel carried. Some even had a lid that closed so that whatever was inside would be protected from wind, rain, sandstorms, and sun.

Now, one thing that was important in a camel rack was for the wood to be free of splinters and smooth to the touch. This was a job that Daniel and Joel did. They would rub each piece of wood with sand, using special gloves so they wouldn't hurt their skin, until each piece was very smooth to the touch.

"Thank you for teaching me how to make God's trees so much better for us to use," said Joel to Amos one day. "No one ever took the time to teach me anything until I came to live with your family." Then he gave Amos a big hug and said, "I love you."

Amos wasn't sure what to say, so he just hugged Joel back. But then Daniel said to Joel, "I know you are probably older than I am, Joel, but you seem like a little brother to me, so I'm going to call you my little brother. And I want you to know that I love you."

From that day forward, both Daniel and Amos called Joel "little brother," which pleased Joel greatly. No one had ever called him a brother before.

This was the best family Joel had ever been a part of.

The day finally came for James, Amos, Daniel, and Joel to load up the camel racks. There were so many that they had to borrow three more carts and ask neighbors to help them. They looked like their own caravan, with the carts stacked so high with camel racks and with four donkeys, four carts, and eight men and boys all in a row on the road.

Joel was in the last cart, so he had a good view of the whole procession. Being part of it was the most exciting thing Joel had ever done.

When they arrived at the caravan camp, there were hundreds of camels and stacks and stacks of trading goods brought to Jerusalem from faraway places, some of which Joel had never heard of. There were bags of spices, bolts of cloth, baskets of all sizes, pottery jars, boots, shoes, bags of fine leather, and all kinds of animal skins.

When the camel racks were unloaded, James spent a lot of time in the main tent working out how he would be paid for his racks. When he came out, he sat down with Amos to explain all that had been said and how everyone had agreed on what the camel driver should give to James as payment. This was all part of training Amos to be a carpenter in the future, and Joel wondered if he could ever be a carpenter too.

"He couldn't pay me all in shekels," James said to Amos, "so we are going to have to take on some trade goods."

James was explaining this because he wanted Amos, as the oldest son, to also learn how to trade the things they made for other goods.

"Here are the things that I agreed to take in exchange for the camel racks we made," James said. "First, the camel driver gave me two baby camels that he doesn't have time to care for. I can take these camels and trade them to a man I know who needs them. The camel drive also gave me some spices that we need, several baskets that your mother can use, and some jewelry and trinkets that we can trade for other things."

"And the most important things the camel driver will give me," James continued, "are fifty treated goatskins ready for use. That is many more skins than I need right now, but they are the best goatskins in the world as they came from high up in the eastern mountains, where the goats live a very hearty life. I told him twenty-five skins was enough, but he said he has not found anyone else who wants the skins, and he does not want to take them on the trip back. He needs to get rid of them to make room for other items that are more valuable to him right now."

"What will we do with so many skins, Father?" Amos asked.

"Well," James said, "I need about twenty-five of them to cut into strips to make straps and fasteners, but I'm not sure what to do with the rest. I don't really have room to store them either."

Upon hearing that, Joel immediately spoke up. "I know exactly what you are supposed to do with those extra goatskins," he said. "If you take them to a street by the temple, I will show you. Then you will see God work another miracle—just like with the dates."

"Well, I guess it wouldn't hurt to go home that way and see what in the world you are talking about, Joel," James said. "Besides, it isn't very far out of the way."

So, while the rest of their makeshift caravan returned home, James, Amos, Daniel, and Joel traveled through the city gate and straight on to the road that lead to the temple. Joel rode in the cart, Amos and Daniel led the donkey, and James walked alongside the cart so he could talk to Joel.

"Tell me where we are going, Joel," James said.

"We are going to see the tailor," Joel said.

"And why are we doing that?" James asked.

"Because the tailor is about to find out that he can trust God to keep His promises."

"Well, we all know that God keeps His promises, Joel," James said.

"I'm not sure you really do know that," Joel said. "I watch all you do for Amos, Daniel, Mother, and me, but I don't see you doing anything for the poor or the needy."

"I don't know any poor or needy," James said.

"That's just what the tailor said, and it didn't take much to remind him that he walks by Old Man every Sabbath, and Old Man is as poor as it gets. Then I reminded the tailor that the Proverbs promise that if we give to the poor, God will repay us. And the tailor gave his best coat to Old Man to keep him warm, so now God is going to pay the tailor back."

James wasn't exactly sure what Joel meant by all of that and how a bunch of goatskins could help the tailor, but he decided he would wait to see what would happen when he got to the tailor's shop.

When they arrived, Joel jumped off the cart and ran into the tailor's store to give the tailor a giant hug.

"Woah," the tailor said. "To what do I owe such a big hug?"

"Because I love you for giving Old Man a brand-new coat, and because God is about to repay you with a brand-new giant blessing."

"And just how is God going to do that, my little friend?" the tailor asked.

"How many wineskins can you sew from one goatskin?" Joel asked.

"Well, if it is a good goatskin, I can sew four regular wineskins from it. And if they are large goatskins, I can sew even more," the tailor answered.

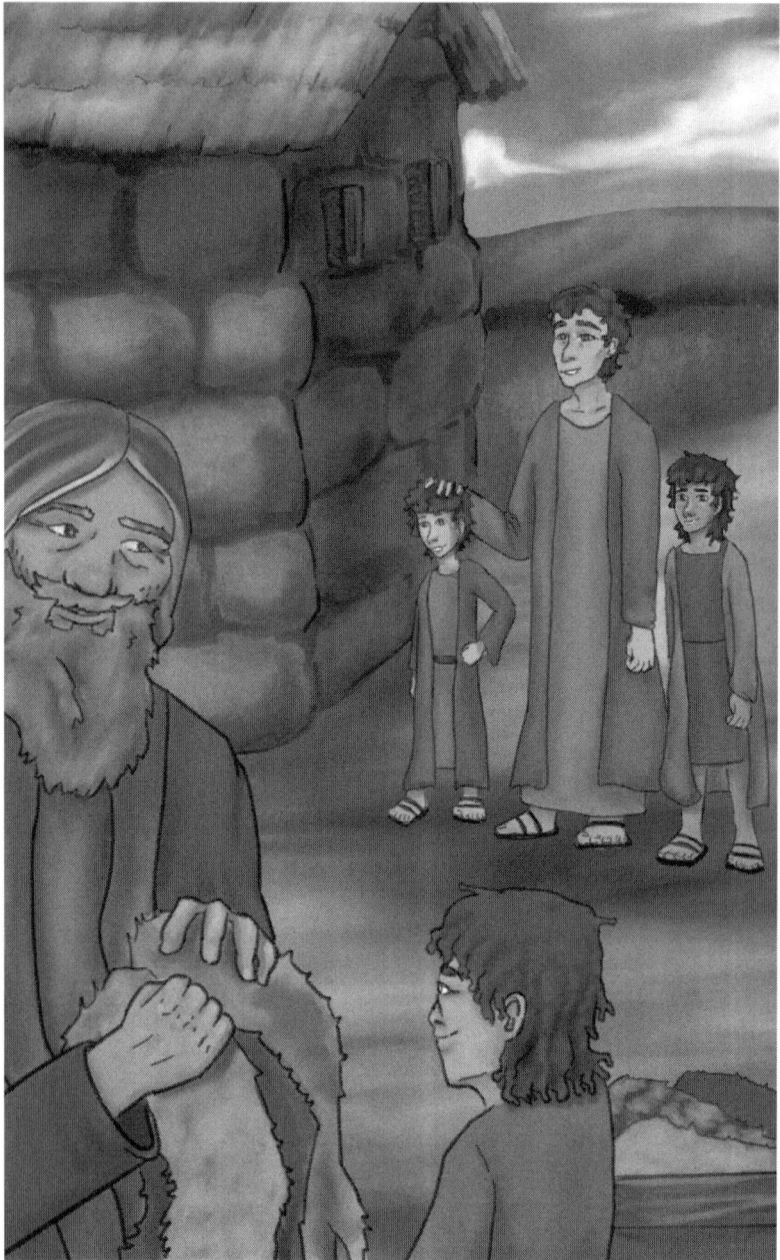

"Come outside," Joel said. "God has sent you twenty-five of the finest goatskins that He makes."

And when he went outside, the tailor saw the finest goatskins he had ever seen.

"Twenty-five of these skins are for you," Joel said, "so you can make at least a hundred wineskins."

"And how much will these fine goatskins cost me?" the tailor asked.

"Nothing," Joel said before James could even speak.

"Why nothing?" the tailor asked.

"Because James told the camel driver he only needed twenty-five skins, and there are fifty in this cart, so the other twenty-five belong to God. They must be what God is using to repay you for giving your best coat to the poor," Joel added. "And when you deliver the order to the wine merchant," he said, "remind him that God is answering his prayer too."

James and the boys were amazed to watch how God was using Joel's faith to do great works for the baker, the tailor, and the wine merchant—not to mention Old Man.

As they left the tailor's shop and started home with the remaining twenty-five goatskins, James said to Joel, "I think I'd like to meet Old Man. Why don't we go see him sometime?"

That seemed like a good idea to Joel, but seeing Old Man took longer than he'd thought it would.

Chapter 6

That night all three boys were saying their prayers before going to sleep. Amos and Daniel had their heads bowed and eyes closed and were praying silently. But Joel was praying out loud with his eyes open.

Amos looked at Joel and said, "Why are you praying out loud and not closing your eyes?"

"I pray out loud so I can be sure God hears me," Joel said. "If I don't pray out loud, then how can God know what I am saying?"

"God knows your every thought, so you don't have to pray out loud," Amos said. "That way many people can pray together and not bother the others in the room who might have trouble thinking with lots of voices around them," he added.

"But if you are the only one in the room praying, then it can be good to pray out loud so others can pray with you," Daniel said.

Before Joel could really think about what Amos and Daniel had said, he asked, "Well, why do you close your eyes?"

"That's easy," Daniel said. "If my eyes are open, I keep thinking about things I'm looking at, but if I close my eyes, I can think only about my prayer and not get distracted by anything else."

The boys continued with their prayers, and when they reached the end, both Amos and Daniel said, "And I pray in the name of Jesus."

Joel heard that and asked, "None of the other families I've been with prayed in the name of Jesus, so why do you?"

"It's because Jesus is in heaven sitting at the right hand of God and telling God what we are praying," Amos said.

"Isn't Jesus your uncle?" Joel asked.

"Yes," Amos said. "He is our father's brother, so that makes him our uncle."

"Then why don't you end your prayers in the name of Uncle Jesus instead of just saying, 'In the name of Jesus'?" Joel asked.

Daniel started to answer, but when he didn't know what to say, he looked at Amos and asked, "Yes, why don't we pray in the name of Uncle Jesus?"

"Well," Amos said, "Jesus is more than just our uncle. He is our Savior and Lord. And besides, if we prayed in the name of Uncle Jesus, it would be saying that we have a special relationship no one else has and that we should get special attention from Jesus. But that is not true. None of us can come before God on our own because of our sin. But Jesus, who had no sin at all, can come right to God on behalf of everyone who has accepted Jesus as Savior and Lord. We can't claim that we are more special to Jesus than everyone else. We can only come to Jesus because of what he did for all men, women, boys, and girls."

"That's a lot to think about," Joel said. "But it sounds good to me, so I'll just start closing my eyes and praying in the name of Jesus too."

After a while, when the boys were under the covers and about to go to sleep, Joel asked, "When are we going to the temple to worship?"

Daniel and Amos just looked at each other, and again Daniel let Amos give the answer.

"We don't go to the temple to worship," Amos said.

"Wow, why not?" Joel asked. "I thought all good Jews went to the temple to worship. Aren't we good Jews?"

"Of course we are Jewish," Amos said. "And we think we are good Jews. But since we follow Jesus as the Messiah, the rabbi and the other Jewish leaders do not let us come into the temple. They do not believe that Jesus is the Messiah."

"So where do we go to worship God?" Joel asked.

"We gather in homes to worship with other people who believe like we do," Amos said. "And we are called the people of the Way." Christianity is, and this is its early beginnings, so I wanted to pose that question.

"I thought that God was only in the temple," Joel said.

"Not anymore," Daniel said, happy that Joel had finally asked a question he knew how to answer. "Since Jesus was raised from the dead, God is now wherever two or three people of the way are gathered together to worship—even if it's in someone's home," Daniel added.

"Can I go with you when the people of the way gather again?" Joel asked.

"We will ask Father if he will let you come," Amos said. And with that settled, all three boys finally fell asleep.

The next morning they were up bright and early. But because it was the middle of the week, they did not go to a gathering of the people of the way. Instead, James gathered the boys and Sarah in the main house kitchen. He looked very serious.

When they were all seated, he told them that for the next three days, they were going to take a very important trip.

"Are you and Amos going to the Sea of Galilee?" Daniel asked.

"Yes," James said. "And the time has come, Daniel, when you should join me and Amos and see exactly what it is we do on these trips."

Daniel was very excited because he had seen his father and Amos make this trip about every third month but was never was quite sure what they did on the trip.

"Are you going to tell me now what you do on these trips, Father?" Daniel asked.

"Yes," James said. "And I want you to listen very carefully because these trips involve some dangers." James wanted Daniel to understand and Amos to be reminded of his explanation.

"After Jesus was raised from the dead and went to sit at the right hand of God the Father, there were many people in Israel who began to believe that Jesus was the long-awaited Messiah that the Jews waited hundreds of years for. But only a few of us believe this. And the rabbi and Jewish leaders see our beliefs as being what they call blasphemies. They say that what we believe is against God, the scriptures, and all Jewish people."

"But aren't we Jewish?" Daniel asked.

"Yes," James said. "But these religious leaders believe we have strayed from the Jewish faith, so they don't want to have anything to do with us. In fact, they wish we would all just go away to another land."

"Well, if they don't like us, why don't we just move away?" Daniel asked.

"Because Jesus told us that we were to stay here in Jerusalem and tell as many people as possible that he died for their sins and that through him they can go straight to God for fellowship. They don't have to go to the rabbi or to the temple anymore."

"Wow, I can see why that would make the religious leaders mad," Daniel asked.

"Well," James continued, "since we have done just that, there are many believers here in Jerusalem, and we meet every week to pray, have fellowship, read the scriptures, and bring in new believers."

"If we don't believe what the religious leaders say," Daniel asked, "why do we read the scripture—or do we have new scriptures?"

"We don't have a new scripture," James said. "We read the same scripture we have always read. Only we now see that all scripture points to Jesus. The religious leaders are blind this truth, so they don't understand what they have been reading all these years."

"So what does all this have to do with the trip we are about to go on?" Daniel asked.

"Since the people of the way have increased in number, there are many people who want to harm us because we threaten their way of life. As we travel to the Sea of Galilee, we will pass through some villages where these people who don't like us live. That's where we need to be careful," James said.

"Then why do we even go?" Daniel asked.

"We go because here in Jerusalem, many of the people of the way are having a hard time feeding their families. The religious leaders have ordered many Jewish people not to buy or sell anything to the people of the way. So we bring back smoked fish from the Sea of Galilee to give to these people and their families," James said. "Because of the danger, I will lead the donkey, Amos will walk along beside the car, and Daniel, you will ride in the cart."

"Can't Joel go with us?" Amos asked.

"I guess so," James said. "But Joel, you need to stay in the cart as well," he added. "Now take the package of food your mother has prepared for us, and let's get started."

The donkey had already been hooked up to the cart, so Daniel and Joel climbed in and sat down on the folds of cloth that would be used to cover the dried fish on their return trip. As they went through the streets of Jerusalem, they had no trouble at all. It was a big enough city, so the people of the way were not yet bothered very much. And they were so good at what they did—like James in his carpentry work, the baker, the wine merchant, and others—that even though some people didn't like what they believed, they still did business with them.

Things changed after James, Amos, Daniel, and Joel left the gates. After a few hours they came to a small village along the road where they stopped at a well to get water and eat some of the food they had brought with them. Almost immediately, a man standing in the doorway of a small house yelled out to some of his friends across the way, "Hey, aren't these some of those blasphemers? What are they doing here? And why are they drinking from our well?"

James ignored them and told the boys to do the same. But the men on the other side of the road started yelling as well. "Get out of our village! We don't want you here," they said. Then more men came out from places in the village, and some even started throwing stones at James, Amos, and the donkey.

Daniel and Joel ducked down so they wouldn't be hit by the stones, and James and Amos started moving the donkey away from the well.

As they moved along, the commotion brought more people out of their homes and out of the fields. All of them were yelling bad things at James and the boys, and many of them were throwing sticks and dirt at them. But James told Amos and Daniel not to fight back. Instead, he told them to pray for God to protect them so they would be able to get the fish that the people of the way needed.

They finally got a good distance away, and the last thing they heard was a man yelling, "Keep away from our village, and don't ever come back. We don't want your kind here."

"That was scary," Daniel said when they finally stopped at a safe place to eat.

"I don't want to go through that village again," Amos said. "It seems much worse than it was the last time, Father. Why do you think that is?"

"As we increase in numbers of people coming to Jesus, we are more of a threat to them. We will take a different route home," James said. Then he added, "If I had known it was going to be that bad, I wouldn't have brought you, Daniel, and certainly not you, Joel."

"I'm sure glad you brought me along," Joel said. "If I hadn't been here, I would have missed out on the joy that I am feeling."

"What are you talking about?" Amos asked. "Where do you find any joy in people throwing rocks at you? Don't you know that those people wanted to hurt us?"

"That's exactly why I have joy," Joel said. "Mother has told me how they treated Jesus before he was hung on the cross, and it seems to me that if people are treating me just like Jesus, it is proof that I am on his side. I'll bet God is really glad about that, so I want to be glad too."

"Father," Amos asked, "is Joel right? Should I be happy to be treated like those people treated us?"

"I need to give that a lot of thought, Amos, before I give you an answer," James said. "I think tonight I'll pray for God to make it clear to me if Joel is correct."

*   *   *

That night, after eating a meal and thanking God for protecting them, the boys went right to sleep. But James sat up before the fire and talked to God about all that had happened that day. He asked God to show him how the people of the way should react to persecution and suffering. By the time the night was over and they were beginning the last leg of their journey to the Sea of Galilee, James had the answer from God.

He told the boys that Joel was correct. That they should be joyful when persecuted for their faith in Jesus as the Messiah and that they should never worry about persecution since God was with them. After all, they knew that God had more power than anyone who might be against them. What's more, like Joel had said, they should consider it a privilege to be treated as Jesus was treated.

*   *   *

Toward the middle of the day, they finally came to the Sea of Galilee. As they approached a small village, Amos seemed to worry about being attacked again. Especially when a few men came up to the cart to speak to them. But right away he learned that he didn't need to be worried.

"Well, well. What have we here?" the first man who approached them said. "Is this the famous carpenter James and his family? So good to see you again. And how is Mary? We pray for her daily. And are these three all your boys? My goodness, they not only keep growing but also seem to be multiplying. I only remember two, but now the two have become three," he said.

"The third came to us recently. His name is Joel," James said.

"Well, Joel," the big man said, "you are in very good company. We are always happy to see your family here as we have so many smoked fish to get rid of. In fact, if you don't take them off our hands, we are all going to feel like we are growing scales."

"You are a funny man, Theodis," James said. "I know for a fact that you, and all the children of Zebedee, have worked long and hard to have fish to give to the people of the way in Jerusalem. Without you, there would be many hungry people in my city."

"It is our very great pleasure," the large man said. And with that, he led them to a stone building where racks and racks of dried and smoked fish were waiting to be loaded into the cart. There were so many fish that they almost spilled out the sides of the cart.

After filling the cart, Amos and Daniel, with a little help from Joel, spread the heavy cloth over the top of the pile of fish. Then they tied it down with new straps that James had made from the goatskins he got at the caravan.

"Boys," James said when they had finished this work, "this cart is so full I don't think it would be wise for you to ride on top of the pile. So Daniel, you and Joel will have to walk alongside the cart with Amos."

This didn't bother Joel at all. It made him feel that much more grown-up.

They said goodbye to all the fisherman who had helped produce this bountiful catch, and God gave them a wonderful trip back to Jerusalem—where there was a big surprise waiting for Joel and James.

Chapter 7

W hen they arrived back in Jerusalem, James and the boys went about delivering fish to the people of the way who needed food. These people included families that were without a father, families where the father's business was suffering because the leaders of the temple had ordered Jews not to buy from them, and houses where people were taking care of orphans. At each house, James, Amos, and Daniel brought the smoked fish inside, but James asked Joel to stay outside.

At one house, an older man named Marcus came out to talk to Joel.

"Hello, young man. How are you this fine day? And what is your name?" he asked.

"My name is Joel, and I'm doing very well because my family is bringing this fine smoked fish to our friends," Joel answered.

"Why are you out here and not inside with the others?" Marcus asked.

"Because James told me to stay here and watch the cart," Joel answered.

"Why does he want you to watch the cart?" Marcus asked.

"I guess to be sure nothing happens to it," Joel said. "Don't you think that is a very important job?" he added, feeling very proud of himself.

"Have you done this at every house you have visited?" Marcus asked.

"Yes," Joel said. "And I am doing a good job of it, too, because nothing has happened at any house while I have been watching the cart."

"I'm sure that is true," Marcus said as he turned to go back inside.

*   *   *

Marcus found James in the kitchen area and asked him, "Why don't you bring Joel into the houses when you make your deliveries?"

This caught James by surprise, and he didn't know exactly how to answer Marcus. The truth was that he didn't know how to explain why Joel was with his family. He wasn't ready to make Joel a permanent part of the family yet, and he didn't want to share that information with everyone. But since Marcus was an elder in the gathering of the people of the way, James took the time to explain everything to him.

"So what you are saying, James, is that because Joel isn't exactly like your two boys, you aren't sure you want to keep him?" Marcus asked.

64

"I guess I never thought of it that way," James said. "Is that bad of me?"

"That is not the right question to ask," Marcus said. "What you need to ask is what God intends for you to do with Joel."

"Well, that is going to take some more prayer on my part," James said.

"Then I'm sure God will make it very clear to you, James," Marcus said.

*   *   *

Having made their final delivery, James and the boys took the last of their fish home to Sarah, and she made them a wonderful supper of date cakes, fish, and dates roasted over the fire. Not a half hour after eating, the boys went to bed exhausted from their long trip.

The next morning, Sarah woke Joel up early and told him she had made a basket of fish and bread for him to take to Old Man. Joel was very excited about that. He had not been back to see Old Man since coming to live with his new family.

With his basket full of food, Joel headed off to the temple to see his friend. When he arrived, sure enough, there was Old Man sitting on the lowest of the steps that went into the courtyard of the temple.

"Old Man! Old Man!" Joel shouted. "Wait until I tell you what has happened to me." Then Joel hugged Old Man very hard and told him that he loved him.

"Slow down," Old Man said. "Just start at the beginning, and tell me everything. As you know, I'm not going anywhere. I've got all day."

So Joel started at the beginning, telling Old Man his story—from the time he followed Amos and Daniel to the caravan right up to when Sarah gave him the basket of food for Old Man.

"That is the nicest thing anyone has done for me since I got my new coat and the fig cakes," Old Man said.

"Hurry up and eat all this food!" Joel said.

"No," Old Man said. "I can't do that. I need to save most of it to eat over the next few days. I don't know when anyone will give me another meal such as this, and I don't want to go hungry."

So Old Man carefully placed most of the food in the bag he always had with him. Then he put the bag on his sled. He and Joel spent the rest of the day just talking and talking.

Finally, Old Man said to Joel, "I hear that James is one of the people of the way. Is that right?"

"Yes, it is," Joel said. "In fact, he is one of the leaders. And he is the brother of Jesus because his mother, Mary, is the mother of Jesus."

"Well then, I have a favor to ask of you, Joel," Old Man said.

"What favor, Old Man?" Joel asked. "Just tell me, and I will do it. You have always been such a good friend. I would love to do you a favor."

"I want to go to one of the gatherings of the people of the way," Old Man said.

"Then you should come with us the next time we worship together," Joel said. "But tell me: What should I tell James about why you want to go?" he asked.

"I never met Jesus," Old Man said. "I tried and tried, but every time I thought I could get near, the crowds were too large, and no one would carry me over to him."

"That's sad," Joel said, "because I'm sure that if Jesus had seen you, he would have healed you like he did so many others."

"I think so too," Old Man said. "But it just never happened. But now I have been listening to people talk as they go in and out of the temple, and they say that the people who are following Jesus, the people of the way, have been used by God to heal just like Jesus healed."

"Wow," Joel said, "that would be so great. As soon as I get home, I'll ask James to bring you to the next gathering."

Joel got up to leave Old Man and go home. But before he had taken even one step, two very big men came down the steps from the temple and grabbed Joel by his arms, lifting him up and starting back up the steps with him in tow.

"Wait, wait!" Old Man shouted. "He is not an orphan. Don't take him. He belongs to a new family."

"Quiet, Old Man," the larger of the two men said. "We say he's an orphan. We saw the family drop him off a couple of weeks ago, and we haven't seen a new family pick him up. So he is an orphan, and we need him to work for us."

"But he does have a new family," Old Man cried.

"If you aren't quiet, Old Man, we will forbid you from begging at the temple ever again," the second man said.

And with that, they dragged Joel away onto the temple grounds.

"Where are you taking me?" Joel asked.

"From now on, you are going to work for us at the temple's stables," the largest man said.

"Did God tell you that I'm supposed to do that?" Joel asked.

"Yeah, yeah," the second man mocked. "We heard directly from God this morning. He told us to go pick up that boy on the steps of the temple and put him to work."

"He sure did," the first man lied. "I heard Him with my own ears."

Joel didn't think they were telling the truth because he was sure that if God wanted him to do this, God would have told Joel as well. But he didn't have any choice but to go along with the men. They were much bigger than him, and they were holding his arms very tightly. At first Joel thought they were taking him into the temple, which he was excited about because he thought maybe God would be there today. But instead, they went out a side gate and down a dirty, dusty path to a stone wall that was higher than Joel's head.

At the wall, they unlocked a wooden gate and pushed Joel through, yelling to someone inside, "We've got a new worker for you, Bushbob." Then they closed the gate, locking Joel inside with no way to get out.

Joel looked around and saw that he was in a filthy stable. It didn't look like the stable had been cleaned in years. There were goats, dirty sheep, and even some oxen, all of which were as big as, or bigger than, Joel. There was manure everywhere and filthy straw in patches all around.

"Well, what have we here?" a man who looked like he had never taken a bath in his life said. "So you are my new worker. I hope you last longer than the previous one. Though you are a strange-looking fella, and you appear as though you have never done a hard day's work in your life."

"You are wrong," Joel said. "I have done really hard work carrying wood and sanding it smooth and walking beside a cart full of fish and sweeping the floor in the wood shop and lots of other chores."

"That's not work," the man shouted. "I'll show you what real work is. Now go to the corner of the stall and start putting all the manure into the wagon."

Before Joel could even move, the big man slapped the back of Joel's head and sent him sprawling on the dirty, messy ground. Lying there on a pile of manure, Joel prayed that God would take care of him and that God would give Joel the strength to work for this man if that was God's will.

*   *   *

Back on the temple steps, Old Man knew he needed to go to the house of James the Carpenter and tell him what had happened. So he picked up his bag, tied it onto his back, lifted his legs up onto his wooden sled, and began the long journey to the carpenter's house. He knew he could make it, but he also knew it would take a long time.

Old Man was used to pulling himself through the streets of Jerusalem on his cart; he had been doing it for his entire life, so his arms and shoulders were unusually strong. But it still took him two hours to get to James the Carpenter's house. When at last he entered the gate to the property, Amos and Daniel were the first to see Old Man. They came running over from where they were helping their mother in the garden and said to him, "Are you the beggar friend of Joel's from the temple? The one he calls Old Man?"

"That I am," Old Man said. "And you must be Amos and Daniel."

"How do you know our names?" Daniel asked.

"Joel spent the entire morning talking all about you," Old Man said.

"Where is Joel?" Amos asked.

"That is what I came to tell your father," Old Man said. "Is he here?"

"Yes," Amos said. "I'll go get him for you."

James came over right away and asked, "Where is Joel, Old Man?"

"They have taken him," Old Man said.

"Who has taken him, and where did they take him?" James asked.

"It was two of the temple workers," Old Man said. "They said Joel was an orphan and that he had to work for them from now on."

"How could they do that, Father?" Amos asked.

"Well, there is a religious law that says if the religious leaders come across an orphan who is not with a family, they have the responsibility to take care of that orphan," James said. "And what really happens is that they put the orphans to work doing very hard labor."

"But Joel is not an orphan anymore," Daniel said. "He is part of our family. Amos and I call him a little brother, and Mother lets him call her Mother."

Just then James realized that Joel was, in fact, a part of their family. He also realized that this was a clear message from God that Joel was now James's son. So James knew he had better do something about the situation.

"What are you going to do, Father?" Amos asked.

"I'm going to get Joel," James said.

"How can you do that when the temple leaders say he is an orphan and they have this rule that allows them to take Joel?" Amos asked.

"Don't worry," James said. "I intend to appeal to a higher authority. While I am gone, Amos, you need to repair Old Man's sled. It's about to fall apart, and the wood is too soft. We have some really hard olive wood that would be just the thing for him to use on his sled."

Having said that, James ran through the gate, headed for the encampment of the Roman soldiers and to his friend the centurion. When he arrived, James explained everything to the centurion. And together, with a half dozen soldiers, they went to the temple to find Joel. Old Man had given them good directions to the stables. When they arrived, the soldiers threw open the gate and demanded that the stable master bring Joel out immediately.

"What are you doing?" the stable master asked the centurion. "You can't do anything here in the temple. It's against your own laws."

"This isn't the temple," the centurion said. "Unless your God now lives in the manure."

"But our law says we can take any orphan off the street and put him to work," the stable master said.

"That may be true," the centurion said, "but this boy is not an orphan."

"I'm sure he is," the stable master said. "I've seen him alone on the steps of the temple."

So the centurion turned to James and asked, "Is this boy an orphan?"

"No," James said. "This boy is my son Joel."

Joel, who had been standing silent at the back of the stable, leapt with joy into the arms of James. He cried out, "Oh, Father! Oh, Father! I love you, Father!"

"Now," the centurion said to the stable master, "if you want to challenge this man who is under the protection of the Roman government, let's all go down to the prison and see who's right and who's wrong."

The stable master, not wanting to go anywhere near a Roman prison, simply said, "Oh, forget it. Just take the boy with you. I'll find me another orphan."

As they left the stable, James thanked the centurion, and he picked up Joel and carried him home.

And for the first time, Joel knew he not only had a family, a mother and a father, but also a real home to call his own. From then on, he called James his father.

Epilogue

Joel was not a person to forget a promise. But Joel was so excited to finally have a father, a mother, real brothers, and a home, that for weeks and weeks he completely forgot about Old Man. But then one day while he was helping Mother in the garden, he looked up and saw Old Man at the gate.

Immediately Joel felt really bad. Was Old Man getting enough to eat? Was he injured in some way? Was he in need of more warm clothes? Joel was almost afraid to find out, but he was so glad to see Old Man that he dropped what he was doing and ran to the gate and gave Old Man the biggest hug he had in him to give.

Joel said loudly, "Old Man, I'm so glad to see you. Are you all right? Do you need anything? Have you enough food? Is everything going okay at the temple?"

"Calm down," Old Man said. "I'm doing just fine. God has been taking care of me, but I no longer beg at the temple."

"Goodness," Joel said. "Why not?"

"It's because I kept telling people at every chance that Jesus is alive and wants to save them and shepherd them. And the religious leaders commanded me to be quiet about Jesus."

"So what happened?" Joel asked.

"I decided that everyone at the temple had their chance, and if they didn't want to hear about Jesus, I would go where people really wanted to hear," Old Man said. "So now I spend time outside the tailor's shop and the wine merchant's shop and the bakery and in the marketplace. People are so much nicer to me at those places than they ever were at the temple. I'm only sorry I didn't leave the temple sooner."

"Why are you here today?" Joel asked.

"Well, in addition to wanting to see you, I was told by the wine-maker that if I wanted a miracle in my life, I needed to go to a gathering of the people of the way and see the elders who meet there. So I am here because I know that James teaches at one of those gatherings, and I thought maybe you could take me there with you the next time you meet."

"Oh, Old Man, I would love to take you," Joel said. "Tomorrow, come to the house of Simon the Potter, and I will meet you there. Do you know where he lives?"

"Yes," Old Man said. "I'll be there by the time the meeting starts." And with that, Old Man began pushing his sled down the road.

The next day James, Sarah, and the boys all went to the house of Simon the Potter to worship, study the scriptures, and have fellowship in Jesus. After the meeting started, Joel kept looking at the door of the house to see if Old Man had arrived. It was already a little after he was supposed to be there, and Joel was afraid that maybe Old Man was not coming.

All of a sudden when Joel looked up, there was Old Man on his sled, right in the doorway. Joel jumped up from where he was sitting in the front row and ran to the back of the house to greet Old Man before Joel's father, James, began to teach.

When Joel got to the door, he gave Old Man a big hug and said, "I love you, Old Man, and I'm so glad you are here today. Come down to the front with me."

"I shouldn't go to the front," Old Man said. "I'm very dirty from pushing my sled so far, and I haven't had a chance to dip in the pool for weeks, so I know I don't smell very good."

"Old Man is right," James, who had followed Joel to the door, said. "He's too dirty to sit with the well-dressed people in the front."

"No, no," Joel said. "He is my friend, and I asked him to come. And he is just as important to Jesus as I am or even you are. And doesn't Jesus accept all of us, no matter how dirty we are in our own eyes? I think when I am with Jesus, I am as clean as I ever am," Joel added.

Upon hearing what Joel said, James was speechless. He realized that Joel was probably right, but he didn't quite agree with Joel himself. However, he did nothing to stop Old Man and Joel from working their way to the front of the room. As they settled in the front row, everyone in the room fell quiet. Then the head elder, Marcus, read verses from Isaiah:

> Then the eyes of the blind shall be opened,
> and the ears of the deaf unstopped;
> then shall the lame man leap like a deer,

and the tongue of the mute sing for joy.
For waters will break forth in the wilderness,
and streams in the desert.

When Marcus had finished reading, he turned to Old Man and said, "Old Man, why are you here?"

"I have prayed to God in the name of Jesus to be healed," Old Man said. "And my friend Joel tells me that when you all gather together, Jesus is among you."

Marcus responded, "Then in the name of Jesus, Old Man, come forward. And will all the elders please come forward as well."

So eleven other men, including James, came forward, and Marcus poured oil onto Old Man's legs. Then Marcus asked all the elders to lay hands on Old Man, and they all prayed that he would be healed of his lameness in the name of Jesus.

While this was happening, two very strange things occurred. First, Joel realized that even though twelve men were praying at once, he could hear and follow each one as if they were the only ones praying. Later, everyone else in the room said they also heard the prayers like this. And then the sled that Amos and Daniel had built for Old Man broke apart right before their eyes. It became nothing but pieces of wood scattered on the ground.

"Oh goodness," Daniel said to Mary, who was sitting between him and Amos. "He won't be able to go back to the city without his sled. And we don't have the tools with us to fix it."

"He will no longer need his sled," Mary said.

And right after she said that, the most amazing thing happened. Old Man leapt up and began dancing around on his two legs as if he had never been lame. And the elders and all the people began to sing and shout and praise God while Old Man ran out the door, crying, "In the name of Jesus, I'm healed! I'm healed! I'm healed! I'm healed!"

Old Man was followed closely by Amos, Daniel, Joel, and many of those in the gathering. Just as the three boys exited through the door, James called out, "Be sure to be home by supper!"

Amos replied, "We will, Father."

*   *   *

After everyone had left, James sat down on the wall just outside the door and thought about all that had happened. As he was thinking, his mother, Mary, came and sat beside him.

"What are you thinking, James?" she asked.

"I'm thinking about how my life has changed ever since Joel came into our home," James said.

"And has the change been for the better?" she asked.

"Very much so," James said. "And you were right, Mother, Joel has taught me many things, and for that I am most thankful," he added.

"And what will you do with what you have learned from God through Joel?" Mary asked.

"Well, one is certain: I will never forget what I've learned," James said.

"And what else?" Mary asked.

"I intend to teach all that I have learned to as many people as I can," James said.

And for the rest of his life, James did just that.

About the Author

Terry Parker was a longtime friend of Larry Burkett, who was heard on over a thousand radio stations with his program *Christian Financial Concepts*. After Larry's death, Terry formed the Larry Burkett Cancer Research Foundation and has written under the pen name GrandDad three other books in a series he calls the Robert P. Rabbit books. These books are primarily given away as an encouragement to children with cancer and other disabilities. Any income from the sale of this book will be used to pay for additional books to be given to cancer camps, children's hospitals, Ronald McDonald Houses, and other places where children with illnesses are ministered to.

Terry is an attorney who retired as a senior partner of a five-hundred-member law firm he was with for twenty-eight years. He is a cofounder of the National Christian Foundation with Larry Burkett and Ron Blue.

Other books by Terry Parker

The Camel Driver's Helper
978-1-7357748-0-0

Sarah's Easter Miracle
978-1-7331023-4-6

A Shepherd's Christmas Story
978-1-7331023-1-5

And Terry Parker as "Granddad"

Katie, Will and the Global Detectives (Book One)
978-0-5781549-9-2

The Moon Rock Mystery (Book Two)
978-0-5781827-5-9

The Treasure of Long John Silver IV (Book Three)
978-0-6921881-2-5